Mr. Wiggle Loves to Read

By Carol Thompson
Illustrated by Bobbie Houser

WATERBIRD BOOKS
Columbus, Ohio

This product has been aligned to state and national organization standards using the Align to Achieve Standards Database. Align to Achieve, Inc., is an independent, not-for-profit organization that facilitates the evaluation and improvement of academic standards and student achievement. To find how this product aligns to your standards, go to www.MHstandards.com.

Children's Publishing

Copyright © 2004 McGraw-Hill Children's Publishing.

This edition published in the United States of America in 2003 by Waterbird Books,
an imprint of McGraw-Hill Children's Publishing,
a Division of The McGraw-Hill Companies
8787 Orion Place
Columbus, Ohio 43240-4027

www.MHkids.com

Library of Congress Cataloging-in-Publication Data is on file with the publisher.

Printed in the United States of America.

1-57768-614-4

1 2 3 4 5 6 7 8 9 10 PHXBK 09 08 07 06 05 04 03

The McGraw·Hill Companies

I am Mr. Wiggle
I'm a book-lover, you see.
There are two main kinds to choose from,
Will you take a look with me?

NONFICTION

There are fiction and nonfiction
Books to go check out.
One on every subject you'll find
I haven't got a doubt.

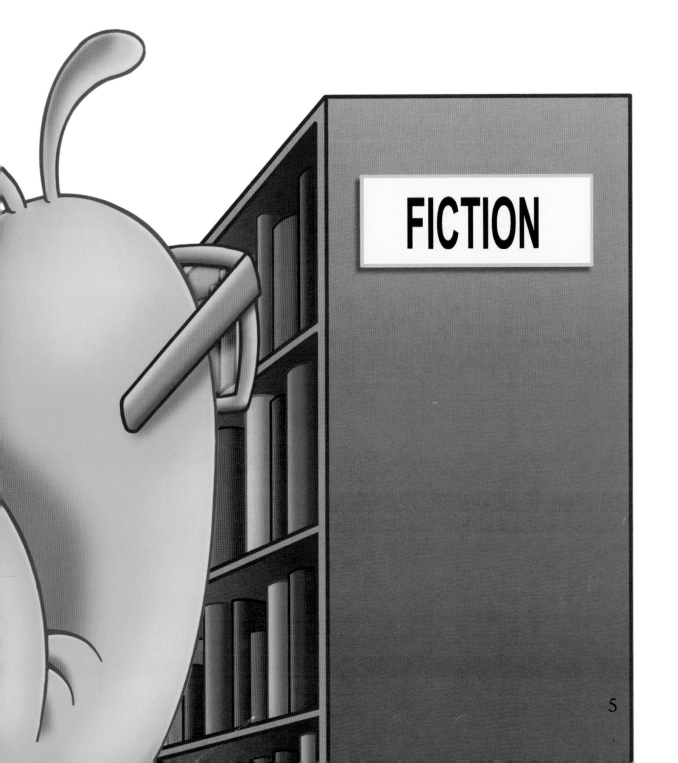

FICTION

Fiction means fake or fantasy,
It also means not true.
These books will tell you stories
I promise that they do.

Once upon a time
in a land far away.

You see, fiction is a tale
Made up in someone's head.
Nonfiction comes from something
That a researcher has said.

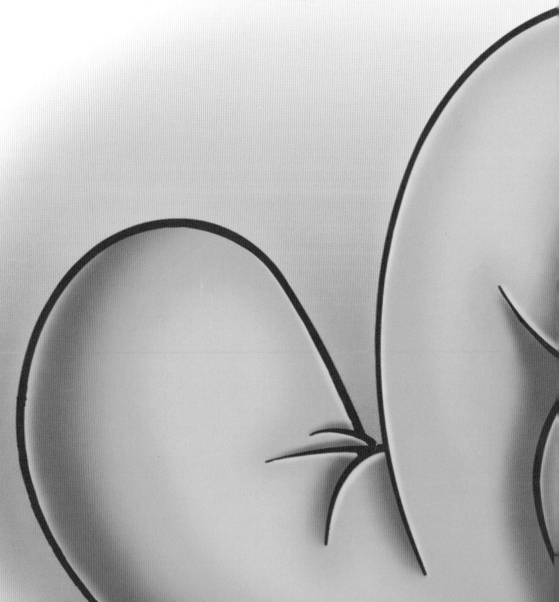

9

Sometimes fiction books are sad
Other times they make you giggle.
But once in a while they even can
Scare poor Mr. Wiggle.

A fiction book could be about
A monster in my closet,
An alien from Jupiter,
Or a dancing cat named Comet.

These books are funny, scary, or sad
Stories for imagination.
You could write a fiction story
That is your very own creation.

Books in fiction are arranged
By the author's name.
Nonfiction books are grouped together
By topics all the same.

BY BRIAN ALLEN

CLARK
ANDERSON

By Dan Atkins

BLACK BEARS

POLAR BEARS

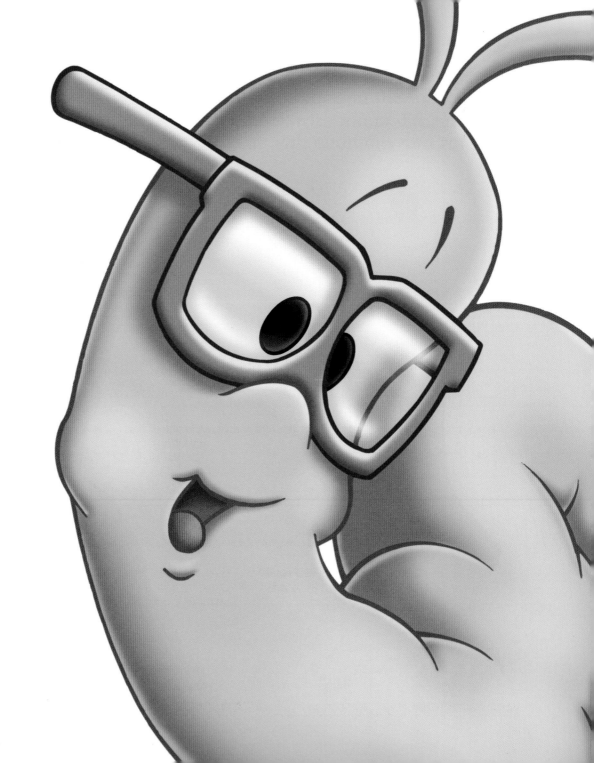

No make believe will there be
In a nonfiction book.
Just facts and figures, truth and data
Will you take a look?

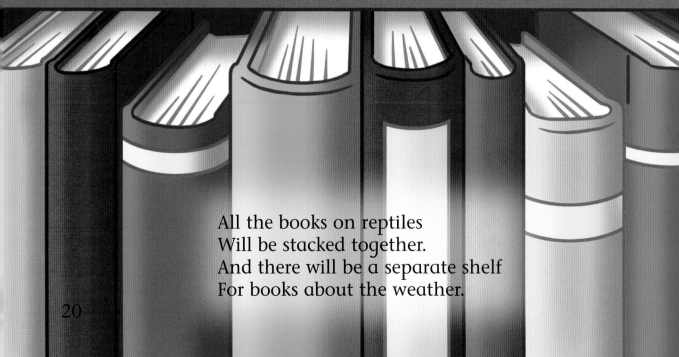

All the books on reptiles
Will be stacked together.
And there will be a separate shelf
For books about the weather.

Nonfiction books are true, you see
They tell facts to make us smart.
They're great for reference or for fun,
I cross my Wiggle heart.

I can read about Lou Gehrig
He was a real hero.
Or I can learn the skills I need
To make my garden grow.

Books about astronauts
In space do interest me.
I also like to read about
This day in history.

Maybe it could be about
The life cycle of a tree.
Perhaps a book on insects
Or on worms that look like me.

It might be about dinosaurs,
Pet care, food, or baseball.
Nonfiction books will show you that
You soon can know it all.

There are so many books in here.
Which one shall I choose?
With fiction or nonfiction
There's no way I can lose!

30

I am Mr. Wiggle,
Your friend, the cute bookworm.
I've just been to the library
And I'm thrilled with what I've learned.

32